Elbert

The Curious
Clock Tower Bear

ANDREW PRAHIN

putnam

G. P. PUTNAM'S SONS

For the supporters
of curiosity—thank you
And for my family—
I cannot thank you enough
— A.P.

G. P. PUTNAM'S SONS • an imprint of Penguin Random House LLC • 375 Hudson Street, New York, NY 10014 • Ⓟ • Copyright © 2019 by Andrew Prahin. • Penguin supports copyright. Copyright fuels creativity, encourages diverse voices, promotes free speech, and creates a vibrant culture. Thank you for buying an authorized edition of this book and for complying with copyright laws by not reproducing, scanning, or distributing any part of it in any form without permission. You are supporting writers and allowing Penguin to continue to publish books for every reader. • G. P. Putnam's Sons is a registered trademark of Penguin Random House LLC. • Library of Congress Cataloging-in-Publication Data • Names: Prahin, Andrew, author, illustrator. • Title: Elbert, the curious clock tower bear / Andrew Prahin. • Description: New York, NY : G. P. Putnam's Sons, [2019] • Summary: Elbert, one of five mechanical bears in the town's old clock tower, has disrupted the proper operation of the clock for the last time, and he is given twenty-four hours to assuage his curiosity about the world below before he will be allowed back in the clock tower. • Identifiers: LCCN 2017011347 (print) | LCCN 2017035331 (ebook) | ISBN 9780525513995 (epub fixed) | ISBN 9780525514015 (KF8/Kindle) | ISBN 9780525513988 (hc) • Subjects: | CYAC: Curiosity—Fiction. | Bears—Fiction. | Clocks and watches—Fiction. • Classification: LCC PZ7.P88646 (ebook) | LCC PZ7.P88646 El 2018 (print) | DDC [E]—dc23 • LC record available at https://lccn.loc.gov/2017011347 • Manufactured in China by RR Donnelley Asia Printing Solutions Ltd. • ISBN 9780525513988 • 10 9 8 7 6 5 4 3 2 1 • Design by Jaclyn Reyes. • Text set in LTC Cloister. • The illustrations were drawn in pencil and colored digitally in Adobe Photoshop.

*T*hrough day and night, for as long as anyone could remember, the town's old clock tower clicked and rattled.

And on the strike of every hour, with bells clanging and pinging, five mechanical bears paraded out for the townspeople below.

Four of the bears took each performance very seriously.

And then there was Elbert, who was filled with curiosity.

At first, Elbert was able to keep his curiosity to himself.

No one seemed to notice when, every once in a while,
Elbert missed a step or let his little lantern drop.

But very early one morning, while the moon still lit the
sky and the town still slept, Elbert spotted something so
magnificent, he couldn't help but stop and stare.

Where had it come from?
What was it doing down there?
And why was it looking up at Elbert like that?

The other bears marched on,
and one by one, they crashed and
piled into a bewildered heap.

The other bears were furious. They couldn't risk Elbert's
curiosity causing an embarrassment while people looked on.
It was decided that Elbert must leave the clock tower.

He would have twenty-four hours to get rid of his
curiosity. Only then would he be allowed to return.

Elbert paused at the base of the tower. As he considered
where to begin, he heard noises coming from a shop he had
only ever seen from far above.

Why not take a quick peek inside?

Elbert watched as a man placed a tray of brightly colored
treats on a table and then disappeared into a back room.

What could those be?
And what was that fantastic smell?

Elbert's eyes opened wide.

How could something taste so much better than rain and snowflakes?
Were all the things around him as amazing as this?

Oh, no! The curiosity!
He had to get out of that shop.

Elbert ran through the town. But at every turn,
he found some new thing that stirred his curiosity.
So he kept moving.

As the sun rose, Elbert reached the edge of a quiet wood. It was there that he formed a brilliant plan. He would lose his curiosity among the trees.

Elbert ducked and dodged through bushes and under branches until he found the perfect hiding spot. Surely, his curiosity would never find him there.

But as he sat perfectly still, Elbert discovered
that the wood wasn't as quiet as it had first seemed.

What was that bird singing about?
It sounded important.
  And what sort of creature was rustling
  through those ferns?
    Shouldn't he go take a look?

Elbert gave up. Curiosity was much too clever
to get lost among the trees.

When the sun was nearing the top of the sky,
Elbert happened upon a stream. Perhaps curiosity
could be washed off.

Fish tickled Elbert's legs as they
swam by. He studied the wiggly path
of the shiny little creatures.

Where were they going?
Were they traveling all the way
to the stream's end?
Did the stream end?

Well, it would seem curiosity couldn't be washed off.

Elbert missed his clock tower friends. He was lost
deep in his thoughts when . . .
A BEAR! It was exactly like Elbert!

It looked very soft.
How soft was it?

Elbert wondered if the bear had knocked the curiosity out of him.

It hadn't.

As the day grew late, Elbert truly started to worry. He still hadn't gotten rid of his curiosity, and time was running out.

He watched clouds brush past the mountaintop above. He wished the wind up there could carry his curiosity away.

Maybe it could.

As Elbert climbed, his mind raced ahead.

If the wind could sweep away curiosity, maybe clouds were actually floating bundles of curiosity.

When it rained, was that a whole bunch of curiosity pouring down on the world?

That made sense, because rain fell on your head and your head was where the curiosity all seemed to gather! Maybe Elbert just had to avoid rain.

Were people with hats less curious? The other bears all had hats. Maybe once the wind swept his curiosity away, he should just get a hat and . . .

Elbert realized that he'd never be rid of his curiosity.

He decided he would hide it. Push it way down.
He would spend every hour going in the most
perfect circles.

Unless . . .

The bears' eyes opened wide.

How could something taste so much
better than rain and snowflakes?
Were all the things around them
as amazing as this?

Elbert thought it was time for them to find out.